SEBASTIAN
and the
BALLOON

To Kenny, Max, and Mickey

Copyright © 2014 by Philip C. Stead

A Neal Porter Book

Published by Roaring Brook Press

Roaring Brook Press is a division of Holtzbrinck Publishing Holdings Limited Partnership

175 Fifth Avenue, New York, New York 10010

Artwork medium: The artwork for this book was created using pastels, oil paints, and pressed charcoal.

mackids.com

Library of Congress Cataloging-in-Publication Data

Stead, Philip Christian, author, illustrator.

Sebastian and the balloon / Philip C. Stead. — First edition.

pages cm

"A Neal Porter Book."

Summary: "When Sebastian launches himself on a journey in a hot air balloon made entirely of Grandma's afghans and patchwork quilts, his boring day turns into the adventure of a lifetime"— Provided by publisher.

ISBN 978-1-59643-930-6 (hardcover)

[1. Voyages and travels—Fiction. 2. Hot air balloons—Fiction.] I. Title.

PZ7.S808566Seb 2014

[E]—dc23

2013044240

Roaring Brook Press books may be purchased for business or promotional use. For information on bulk purchases please contact Macmillan Corporate and Premium Sales Department at (800) 221-7945 x5442 or by email at specialmarkets@macmillan.com.

First edition 2014

Book design by Philip C. Stead

Printed in China by South China Printing Co. Ltd., Dongguan City, Guangdong Province

1   3   5   7   9   10   8   6   4   2

SEBASTIAN and the BALLOON

PHILIP C. STEAD

A NEAL PORTER BOOK
ROARING BROOK PRESS
NEW YORK

SEBASTIAN sat high on his roof—something he was never supposed to do. "There is nothing to see on my street," he thought. "Nothing to see at all."

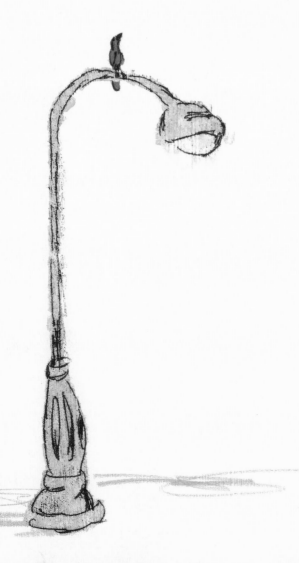

"Tonight I'll leave and see something new for a change."

So Sebastian gathered all the things he would ever need.

And when night fell, Sebastian boarded the balloon he'd built
from Grandma's afghans and patchwork quilts.

He charted a course. He checked the breeze. He cut the strings . . .

and floated free.

Soon it was time for a snack. Sebastian landed his balloon beside a leafless tree.

"Excuse me," asked a bear, "are you a real balloon pilot?"
"Of course I am!" replied Sebastian. "Are you a real bear?"
"Of course I am!" replied the bear.
The two looked each other right in the eyes.
"Would you like a pickle sandwich?" asked Sebastian.

The wind picked up and soon it was time to go—
up and up and into a milky gray fog.
"Can you see the end of my nose?" asked the bear.
But before Sebastian could answer there came a loud POP!

And they fell down, down, down—out of the fog and onto the roof of a ramshackle house.

"I'm sorry," said a very tall bird. "It was my fault."

"It's okay," said Sebastian. "Would you like a pickle sandwich?"

Three sisters called out, "What are you doing up there, up on the roof of our house?"

"Our balloon has sprung a leak," answered Sebastian.

"Oh, dear," said the sisters. "If only we could find our knitting needles . . ."

Luckily, Sebastian had all the things he would ever need.

So the sisters could start their mending.

"You must be having such fun," they said, making loops and tying careful knots of yarn. "It's been so long since we've traveled. When we were very young we'd pack strawberry sandwiches and climb up over the mountain. On the other side is the most perfect roller coaster you will ever see."

Soon the knitting was done.

And when the wind picked up,
everyone knew it was time to go . . .

up and over the mountain to the most perfect roller coaster they would ever see.

But the paint was chipped and faded. The beams were bent and broken. The loop-the-loop leaned badly to one side, and flocks of squawking pigeons roosted up and down the track.

"Oh, no!" cried the sisters. "This is not right, not right at all!"

Luckily, Sebastian had all the things he would ever need.

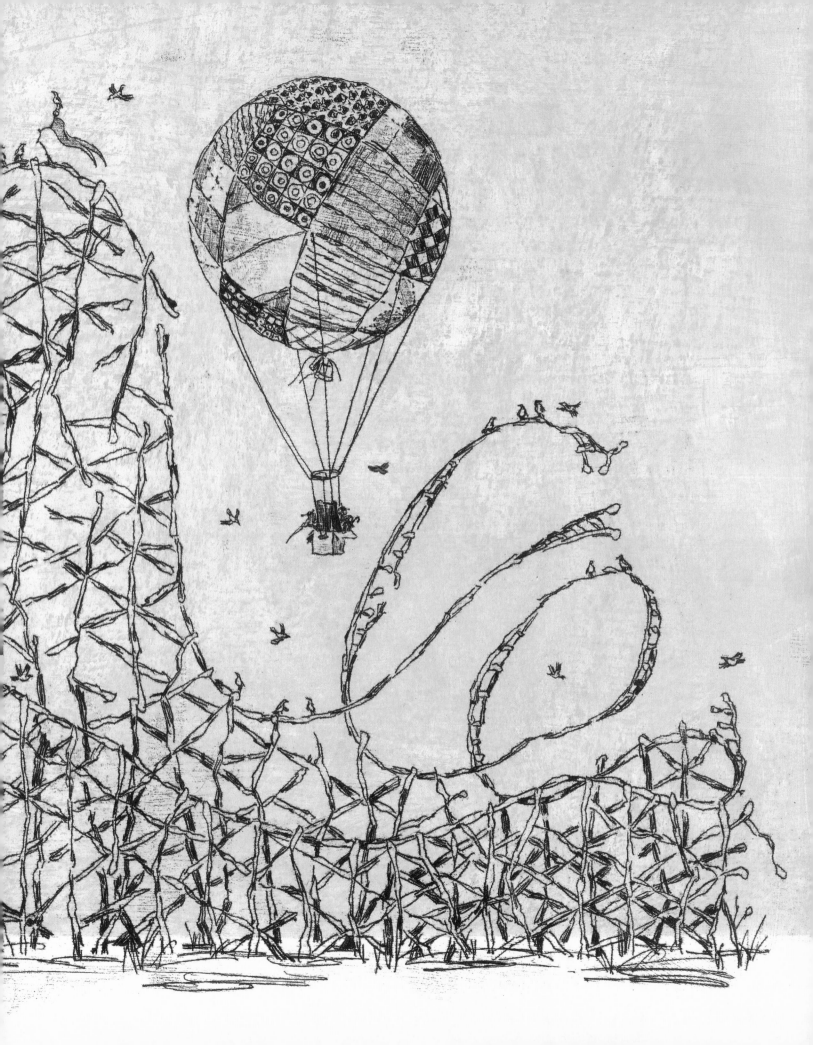

"So we'll polish and paint!
We'll hammer and nail!
We'll pull with all of our might!"

"And last we'll look the pigeons right in the eyes and say—

GO AWAY!"

And the pigeons flew off,
all the way to the leafless tree.

And the tree was glad to have company.

"Good work!" said the sisters.
"Well done!" said the very tall bird.
"Amazing!" said the real bear.

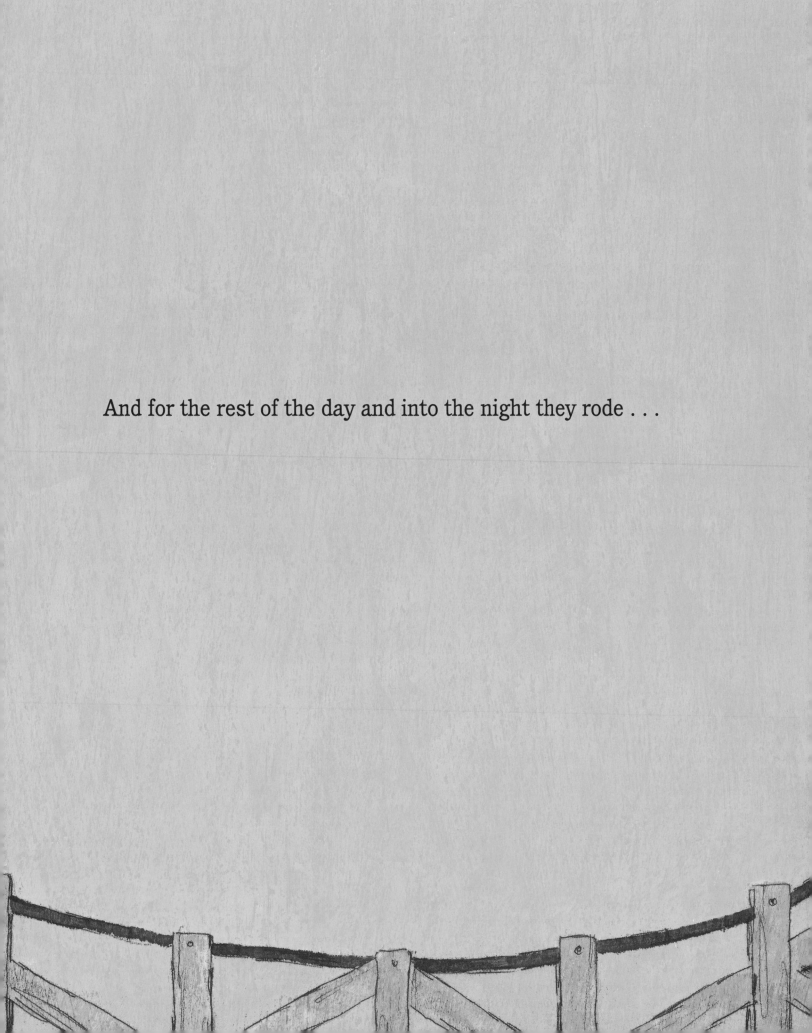

And for the rest of the day and into the night they rode . . .

and rode . . .

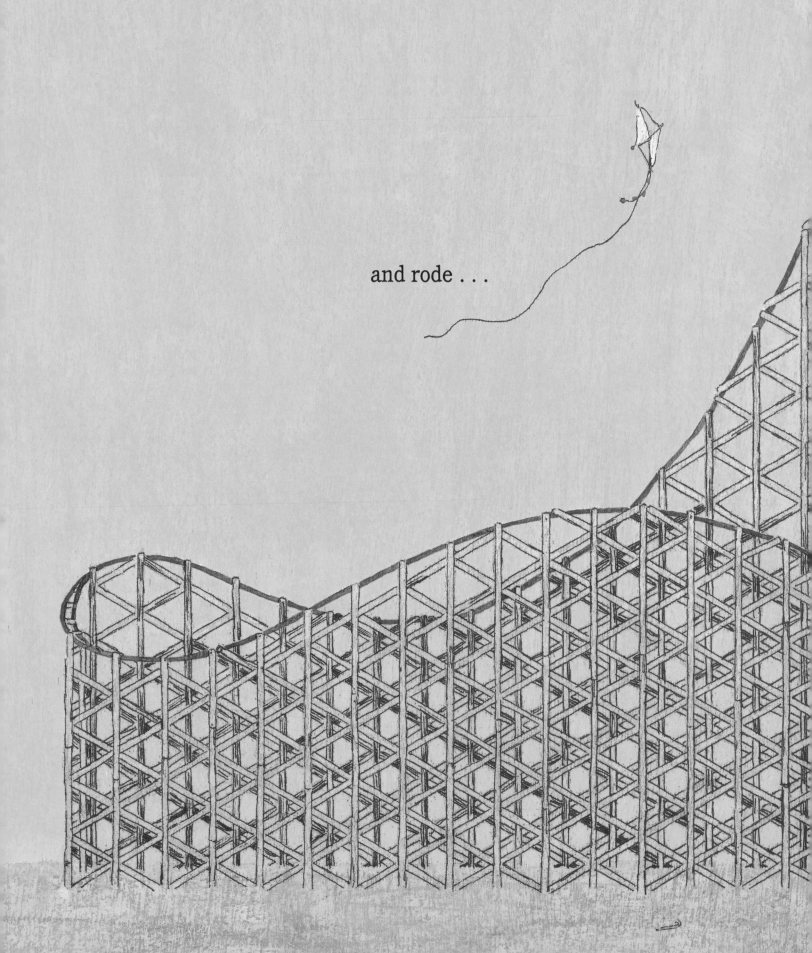

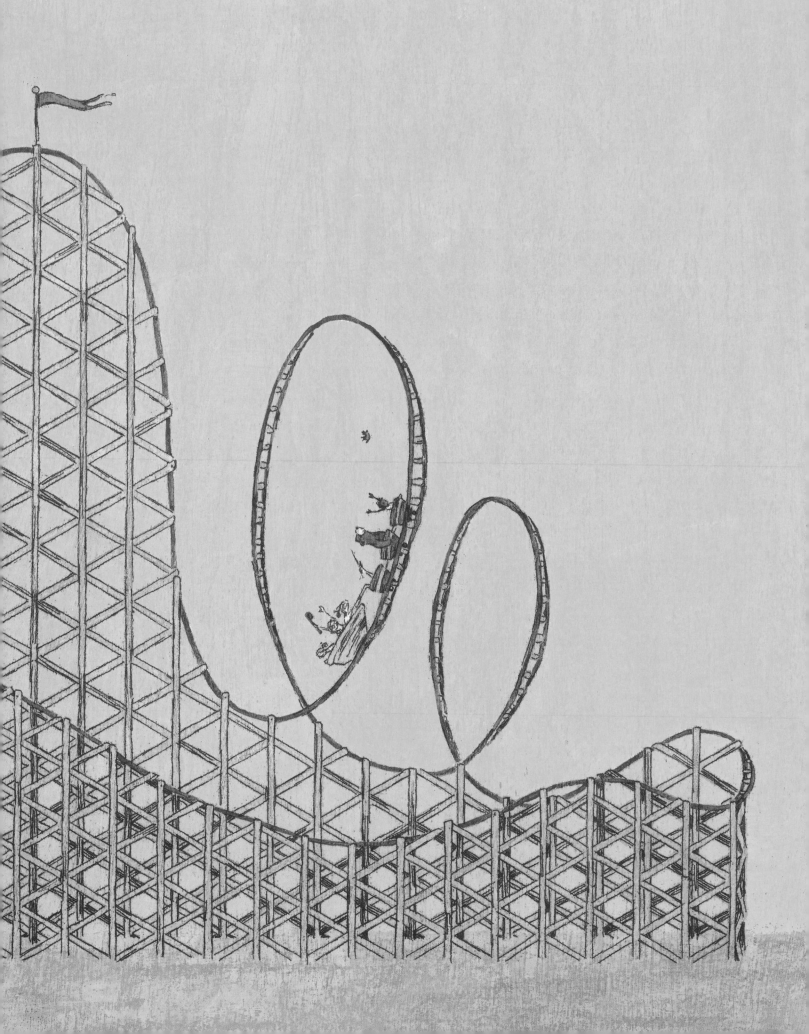

until the wind picked up and it was time to go.